POT LUCK

Remembering Manya Reicin Rosenberg ("Mama Joe")   *—TT*

•

For Aviva Ann Musicus with love from Grandma   *—NLM*

Text copyright © 1993 by Tobi Tobias
Illustrations copyright © 1993 by Nola Langner Malone
All rights reserved. No part of this book may be reproduced or utilized in any form or by any means, electronic or mechanical, including photocopying and recording, or by any information storage and retrieval system, without permission in writing from the Publisher. Inquiries should be addressed to Lothrop, Lee & Shepard Books, a division of William Morrow & Company, Inc., 1350 Avenue of the Americas, New York, New York 10019. Printed in the United States of America.

First Edition   1 2 3 4 5 6 7 8 9 10

Library of Congress Cataloging in Publication
Tobias, Tobi. Pot luck / by Tobi Tobias ; illustrated by Nola Langner Malone.
p.   cm. Summary: Rachel learns her grandmother's definition of "pot luck" when she helps Gram prepare dinner for an old friend. ISBN 0-688-09824-X.—ISBN 0-688-09825-8 (lib. bdg.) [1. Grandmothers—Fiction. 2. Cookery—Fiction. 3. Jews—United States—Fiction.] I. Malone, Nola Langner, ill. II. Title. PZ7.T56Po 1993 [E]—dc20
92-27678 CIP AC

POT LUCK

by Tobi Tobias • illustrated by Nola Langner Malone

Lothrop, Lee & Shepard Books   New York

When the phone rings, it's Gram's friend Sophie. Sophie lives in the country—the cows and trees country—but a long time ago she and Gram both lived in the Old Country, away over the ocean where they spoke a different language. When I stay with Gram, she tells me all about her friends and some of them come to visit us, but I've never met Sophie. She lives too far away.

"No, no, Sophie," Gram is shouting into the phone. "Today is fine. Perfect. You'll come to dinner. Of course you'll come to dinner. No, I don't mind such short notice. The only thing is, you'll have to take pot luck."

"What's pot luck, Gram?" I ask her after they finally decide six o'clock and hang up.

"When a guest comes at the last minute and eats whatever the family has in the house. Hurry up and get your shoes on, Rachel, we're going shopping."

"But—"

"And don't forget to take a sweater."

At the butcher's, Mr. Fleissner says, "Mrs. Gold, I have got the perfect chicken for you," but Gram pokes and sniffs it anyway to make sure.

The fruit and vegetable lady brings Gram the best apples and carrots, onions and parsley from the just-unpacked crates in the back of the store. I'm picking out the crispiest, greenest cucumbers from a whole mountain of them, the way Gram taught me, but the lady says, "Not those, sweetheart," and disappears into the dark back room again.

In Hershel's dairy Gram buys fresh eggs, lifting them out of their pockets one by one to check for cracks.

Gram walks past the bakery like always, without even looking in the window.

"Cake should not be store-bought," Gram says.

In the supermarket she shakes her head, like always, over the food wrapped up in plastic and buys stone-ground flour—"Make sure the bag doesn't leak, Rachel"—brown rice, a sack of tiny, dried, green peas, and another sack of yellow ones.

While we're waiting in the check-out line, I ask her, "Gram, I thought you said pot luck meant—"

"It's nice to add a few little extras when company's coming. Now watch to see they ring up the prices right."

In the kitchen we start on the cake first so the oven will be free later for roasting the chicken. Gram stirs up the batter with her big wooden spoon and lets me beat until my arm gets tired.

"Count the strokes, Rachel. Three hundred—no more, no less."

"Is it Sophie's birthday, Gram?"

"Oh, we old ladies don't have birthdays," Gram says.

"Then why—"

"Count, sweetheart."

When the cake is in the oven, we wash the peas for the soup. Gram rattles them back and forth—green and yellow—in her metal strainer.

"Pick out any bad ones, Rachel. Your eyes are sharper than mine."

When the soup starts bubbling in the pot, we slice the cucumbers see-through thin, put them in their vinegar-and-sugar bath, and press them down with a heavy plate.

Then I cut up apples into tiny bits; Gram soaks the raisins and cooks the rice. Next those three things get mixed together and stuffed into the chicken, and the chicken gets stuffed into the oven as the cake comes out to cool.

"Gram, why are we making such a fancy dinner?"

"To teach you, sweetheart," she says, giving me a kiss on top of my head, "so you'll know how when you need to."

Gram and I wash all the dirty bowls and clean the
stove and the sink and scrub the kitchen counters.

"Take a dry towel and polish the faucets," Gram
says, mopping the floor.

In the living room Gram dusts with her special

cloth and plumps up all the cushions and makes sure
everything's neatly in its place.

    I remind her, "You dusted yesterday, Gram."

    "How would you like to run the vacuum cleaner?"
Gram says.

After we give the soup another stir and the chicken another good basting, we sit down for a little rest. Gram tells me about the Old Country, when she and Sophie were young.

"We were raised together, like two chicks under one hen. Sophie and Reba, Reba and Sophie— together day and night. Even when the boys started looking at us, we were still friends, even if they were all after Sophie first."

"Why did they like Sophie best, Gram?"

"Well, my mama said it was because she could cook and sew and keep a house shining. But if you took one look at her, Rachel, you knew it wasn't for that. Sure, she could sew. She could cook. Everything— wonderful. But it was something else, I promise you. Oh, how she could dance and sing. When Sophie was

dancing, that long, red hair would go flying around her...."

"She had red hair, Gram?"

"Red hair, blue eyes, and a smile like sun in the morning. The thing I could never figure out was, when your grandpa came to our town from Lublin—that was the town over the way—why he picked me. He never even looked at Sophie once."

Another stirring—Gram sips some of the steaming soup from the ladle and adds two tiny pinches of salt—and one more basting, and then we go out to the backyard, where the rosebush is still making giant pink roses, even though it's September. Gram lets me choose which roses are ready to pick and even lets me cut them with the sharp kitchen scissors. Meanwhile she carries her fold-up chair into the last patch of sun and calls Koshka onto her lap and brushes him until his creamy fur shines.

"Could we put a bow on Koshka," I ask Gram, "the way we did on his birthday?"

"Now we don't want to go making things so special," Gram says. "Put those flowers in some water, darling, and watch out for thorns."

Next we go into the dining room and cover the
table with the linen cloth that's too heavy for one
person to unfold alone. We put out the good plates—
the ones with gold on the scallopy edges—and the
glasses with the diamond pattern cut into them.

"Be careful," Gram says, once for each glass.

The silver knives and forks and spoons have the
first letters of her mother's three names laced

together on them—RML. Gram rubs each one on her apron and sets it exactly in place. In the middle of the table she puts a deep red glass vase and stands the roses up in it; they make the whole room smell flowery. We step back to admire the table, then Gram steps back to look at me.

"Pot luck doesn't mean blue jeans," she says, and marches me upstairs.

Gram puts on her fancy blue silk dress. On the collar she pins the brooch Grandpa gave her when they were sweethearts in the Old Country. She brushes and combs her white hair until it looks like tiny, curling ocean waves, then does it up with ten silvery hairpins.

She takes my hair out of its old, messy braids and brushes and combs and twines it into new, sleek braids with red ribbons twisting through them all the way to the ends. She tucks my blouse tighter into the waist of my skirt and looks me up and down. She says, "There, now," and "Did you pick up your room?"

The doorbell rings and it's Gram's friend Sophie. Gram and Sophie give each other a hug and a kiss and another wraparound hug.

"This is my Rachel," Gram says. "She doesn't speak any Yiddish, but otherwise she is perfect."

"A *shayne maydele*," Sophie says, which I know is Yiddish for "pretty little girl."

Sophie is beautiful. Her face is all crinkly with wrinkles, and her eyes are blue, blue, blue.

She has a knobbly parcel in one hand, a damp, lumpy one in the other, and a box wrapped in fancy paper tucked under her arm. The knobbly parcel turns out to be a homemade cheese, and the damp one is a Swedish ivy plant.

"Give it lots of sun and enough water," Sophie warns Gram, "and it'll grow more than you want, even."

"Girls still like to play with dolls sometimes, don't they?" she asks, handing me the box.

The soup is hot and thick and delicious. Gram
carves the chicken and ladles brown chicken gravy
over the stuffing. The cucumber slices are icy and
crunchy, sweet and sour. Gram pours out golden wine
into three tiny thimble glasses. We have to rest before
we eat the cake.

"Oh, it's wonderful, too much, you shouldn't have bothered," Sophie says, over and over.

"It was nothing, nothing," Gram answers, brushing away compliments. "Have another little bit. You've hardly eaten anything."

When we can't eat one bite more, we clear the table and make tea. Sophie looks at the tea leaves in the bottom of my cup and says, "I'll tell your fortune, Rachel."

And she does. "You will travel around the whole wide world until you are ready to come home."

"Tell Gram's," I say to Sophie.

Sophie's blue eyes study Gram, and a little smile dances around her lips.

"You will live to be a hundred, Reba," Sophie promises Gram.

It gets so late that Sophie has to stay all night. Gram gives her her bed and comes to sleep with me.

We put on our nightgowns and take turns in the bathroom. I braid Gram's hair for the night, and she braids mine.

We lie down close together in my bed, with me on the wall side and Gram on the outside so I won't fall out. The doll Sophie brought me is tucked between us so she won't be afraid on her first night.

"No story now, it's so late," Gram says. Before I can beg, she promises, "Two tomorrow," and settles down to sleep.

The good smells of dinner are still in the house, and it is so quiet you can hear Koshka purring.

"Gram…?"

"Ja, sweetheart?"

"I thought you said pot luck meant whatever we were having anyway."

"A woman like Sophie Paderewski," Gram says,
"you don't feed last night's stew."